WARNING

This book contains sexually explicit scenes and adult language. It may be considered offensive to some readers. This book is for sale to adults ONLY.

* * * * * * * * * * * * * * * * * *

Please store your files wisely where they cannot be accessed by underage readers.

ISBN-13: 978-1987863949
ISBN-10: 1987863941

Other Books by Darla Dunbar:

<u>The Romeo Alpha BBW Paranormal Shifter Romance Series</u>

Amanda Walker thinks that she has a normal and boring life. That is until after her 24th birthday. Everything changes when she meets the man who says he was supposed to be her husband. Denying everything the man says, she fights him every step of the way. But after he kidnaps her, Amanda discovers that there are some things about her family that her parents kept a secret all these years. Among the history of the family she learns secrets she thought only happened in story books. Can Amanda tell the difference between truth and lies or is she this mysterious woman that holds the key to a legacy?

<u>Romeo Alpha Blood Lines Romance Series</u>

Twenty-four years have passed in relative peace for Amanda and Romeo. They've raised five children into adulthood and are thoroughly enjoying their lives as the Alpha King and Queen of the werewolves. At twenty-four, Sarina is just stepping into her powers and will be ripe for mating when her birthday comes in two weeks. What no one knows is the danger that lurks just outside their tight knit community. Romeo has made peace with the other clans and has enjoyed that peace, but it will all come crashing down around him when his oldest daughter comes of age to take a mate.

<u>The Alpha Feud BBW Paranormal Shifter Romance</u>
<u>Series</u>

Eliza's life consisted of reporting on boring, crowd-pleasing events, like their country livestock fair. With the arrival of two handsome brothers, the lives of Eliza and her best friend, Melissa, are shaken to the core. For Eliza, the arrival of this new man becomes a test of her relationship with her current boyfriend, who she's been happily living with for over six years. Does Hayden, a complete stranger, really wield the power to make Eliza reconsider her relationship with Andrew?

<u>The Alpha Packed BBW Paranormal Shifter</u>
<u>Romance Series</u>

Darlene has led a quiet life since suffering through a terrible break-up. She wants nothing more than to spend her time in front of the TV, away from any sort of trouble. But all that goes down the drain when handsome, rugged and rough Idris comes into her life. He is a werewolf on the lookout for his missing pack leader. Darlene quickly finds herself pulled towards this mysterious man and at the same time finds herself falling deeper and deeper into the world of the supernatural.

<u>The Mind Talker Paranormal Romance Series</u>

Ananda finds herself on the run and she's not alone. With help from Jared, a stranger that she just met, the two evade capture by an organization that is intent on hunting her kind. Ananda and Jared are able to read minds. When an unfortunate incident happened involving a disturbed individual that resulted in the death of his schoolmates, the secret organization decided to take action.

<u>The Leather Satchel Paranormal Romance Series</u>

Valtina is stuck in Middle World, unable to pass on to The Afterlife. In order to redeem herself from past deeds done, she must help bring romance back into the world and stop The Dark Side from destroying love in its entirety. Following orders issued by Ladaya and armed with a leather satchel filled with the appropriate tools and weapons, Valtina embraces each mission with enthusiasm.

Get the latest update on new releases from the author at:

https://darladunbar.com/newsletter/

This book is Part Ten of "<u>The Daemon Paranormal Romance Chronicles</u>"

Book 1 - The Awakening

Phoebe grew up not knowing her mother. The stranger, Apollo Mikos, claimed to know her mother. After that day, Phoebe's life would change forever.

Book 2 - The Shifter

Phoebe is surprised when her dog, Ace, shows up from nowhere. She is on a mission with Apollo to kill the Qilin. That is the only way that the true leader of daemons will emerge.

Book 3 - Forgotten

Juno has been stirring up trouble that has prolonged the infighting among the daemons. In order to get her to stop, Phoebe agrees to give up a year of her memories. But making deals with a siren is never a good thing. Without her memories, Phoebe's romantic relationship with Supay no longer exists. Instead, she leaves Supay for Apollo.

Book 4 - The Siren's Trap

The unsuspecting couple, Phoebe and Supay, made a deal with Juno to stop the infighting among the daemons. But at what price? An entire year was wiped clean from Phoebe's mind. Now Phoebe was with Apollo. Desperate to get her back, Supay considers Juno's new deal. Is it worth the price to pay for the dubious result? To win back Phoebe's love, Supay will need to be unfaithful to her.

Book 5 - Exposed

Hiding away in Peru, Supay and Phoebe start their own family, away from the chaos and the daemon infighting. Meanwhile, Apollo, heart-broken and lost, is lured into another one of Juno's schemes. Making deals with a siren never turns out right. If Apollo accepts the deal, the love of his life may resent him for the rest of his natural life. If he doesn't take the deal, she is lost to him forever.

Book 6 - The Beginning

As preparations for the war between daemons are underway, everyone must begin to choose. Siding temporarily with Apollo, Juno has a moment to look back on her life and figure out how she arrived at this moment. As she sifts through memories of the past, a specific dark stranger stands out. How far will young Juno go with her new love? More importantly, will her mother, Circe, discover the secret tryst?

Book 7 - The Treachery

Having broken the cardinal rule of the sirens, Juno must take action to save her own life and the life of her unborn child. In order to keep her secret safe from the sisterhood, she must kill her lover and conceal her shame. Will Juno betray the sisterhood and save her lover or will she remain loyal by slaying him instead?

Book 8 - Duplicity

Juno's mother, Circe, discovers her lies and gives her an ultimatum to fix everything. As Juno races against the clock to protect her loved ones from Circe, she makes a final choice that could leave her perpetually unhappy. Left to wander the world alone, Juno realizes that freedom means nothing if there is no one to share it with. The nature of Juno's vendetta—and the means she achieves it with—are finally revealed.

Book 9 - Reconnaissance

As Juno's hunt for the daemon's fortress unfolds, Apollo is left alone wondering if she will truly return to him. Will Juno be able to resist her base instincts? More importantly, will she be able to get to the fortress and return without being spotted? Discover how Juno's stealth mission works out.

Book 10 - The Interrogation

Juno tries to hide her rising fear in the presence of her captors. As her fear mounts, she holds on to the hope that Phoebe or Supay will take pity on her. Before that can happen, she has to come clean to Supay about her past. Could he possibly forgive her for what she has done? Will Juno remain faithful to Apollo or will her siren urges take over? Discover how the confrontation with Supay unfolds.

The Daemon Paranormal Romance Chronicles

The Interrogation

Book Ten

By Darla Dunbar

Copyright Revelry Publishing 2015

Table of Contents

Chapter One..1
Chapter Two 6
Chapter Three 11
Other Books by Darla Dunbar.................................50
About the Author - Darla Dunbar 51
Connect with Darla Dunbar....................................52

Chapter One

WITHIN THE inner recesses of the cave fortress, Supay was struggling to get everything under control. The impending war with the Roman daemons had everyone on high alert and each Greek daemon had been called to the fortress. Unfortunately, this meant that undesirable creatures like Cleonae had also been brought into the fold. Supay tried to hide his disgust in dealing with these creatures, but found it almost impossible.

After a long day at the fortress, Supay was finally getting a chance to go to bed. Entering the bedroom, he saw Phoebe on the bed. Since Peru, she had been different. Everything had been going perfectly for a while. Once her memories had finally recovered, she had returned from Spain and become the perfect mate for Supay. They had enjoyed living blissfully together with their daughter, Irene, until everything changed one day. At first, Supay thought that he had imagined the change. Little things that Phoebe did seemed different. Over the last few months, he had realized the unfortunate truth: Phoebe had found out about the deal with Juno. Now, she was unable to love him as fully and completely as she had before. Despite this realization, Supay did not do anything to change the situation. He hoped that he was wrong and did not want to make things worse if Phoebe truly did not know.

Hearing Supay enter the room, Phoebe rolled over. "Hey, love. How is everything going? I just put Irene to bed." She smiled and patted the bed invitingly.

Removing his clothes, Supay slid into bed next to her. Although it appeared like most fortresses on the inside, the underground complex became extremely chilly at night. Supay was glad that he could share the bed with Phoebe each night. Rolling toward her, he gently looped her hair behind her ear. "Preparations are underway, although it could always be better. I just wish that we could tell exactly what the Romans are up to right now."

Next to him, Phoebe remained silent. She had avoided telling Supay about Juno. Phoebe knew that Juno had once dated Supay and also knew that Juno was the reason their relationship was starting to fall apart. If Supay knew that Juno was interrogated and tortured in the dungeon, he would never forgive her. Phoebe winced. The torture had not been intentional. She had thought that Cleonae's natural inclination to capture and keep damsels meant that he would protect them. This obviously was not the case. The sadistic Nemean lion daemon had merrily started the interrogation.

Noticing her expression, Supay raised an eyebrow. Something was off, but he did not know what it was. "Phoebe?" he asked.

Distracted from her thoughts for the moment, Phoebe realized that Supay knew she was keeping a secret. She would have to distract him for the moment. "Nothing, Supay, I was just thinking. Wait here." Slipping out of bed, Phoebe went into the closet and found her favorite lingerie. Sliding her body into the black lace, she stepped back and admired her figure. All she needed now was some shoes and possibly lipstick.

After applying a coat of dark red lipstick that matched beautifully with her hair, Phoebe smoothed her hair back into a tight bun. She slipped into tall, black boots. Before leaving the closet, she slipped some elbow-length, black gloves over her hands and arms. She was ready.

Exiting the closet, Phoebe flipped on the music player. Slow-paced, ethereal music flooded the room as she turned on a lone red lamp. Around her, the bedroom had been transformed from a typical sleeping area into a dominatrix's den. Smiling, she walked up to the bed. Supay had remained exactly where she had left him. She motioned for him to spread his arms and legs toward each bed post. Pulling out the bed restraints, Phoebe roped his arms and legs to individual bed posts.

Beneath her, Supay flexed his muscles. The restraints were strong. He watched every move that Phoebe made and waited for her to give him an order. Recently, they had started to expand their sexual tastes. Bondage had become one of their favorite games to play. He enjoyed having her as his mistress because it gave him an opportunity to watch her body smoothly flow against his.

Next to him, Phoebe had placed an ice cube in her mouth. She eyed Supay for a moment. Every fiber of his body ached for her to touch him and she knew it. Leaning down, she traced her mouth and the ice cube along his chest. As her mouth stopped at his nipple, Supay groaned. The coldness was excruciating, but he wanted her to touch him so terribly. Pushing his body toward her, he tried to get her to touch him more fully.

Phoebe smiled. This is what she enjoyed the most. She loved the element of control and the enjoyment that came from teasing him. Gently holding the ice in her mouth, she allowed it to run a cool trail down his body. Next to his cock, she stopped. Reaching out with her hands, she stroked along the hard contours of his member until Supay began dripping pre-cum. Within her artful hands, Supay writhed and moaned. More than anything, he wanted her to continue or to release him. After ensuring that Supay was fired up, she dropped her head down to the tip of his cock and opened her mouth. As she took him fully into her mouth, the coldness of the ice stung Supay and caused him to jerk backward. Despite an intense desire to escape from the cold, he pushed back into her mouth as she took him deeper.

Groaning, Supay could not stop himself from thrusting into her mouth. The coldness and the extended tease had brought him to full attention. All he wanted was for her to take him. Seeing his excitement, Phoebe grinned in wicked pleasure. Her evening of teasing was not over yet. Removing the ice, she straddled his body and slipped off her panties. Instead of letting him enter her, she spread the lips of her cunt over either side of his cock lengthwise. Rubbing against him, she allowed him to feel the moist exterior of her cunt as she moved her body against his. Supay moaned in excruciating agony as she pressed her body against his.

As she moved her hips, Phoebe's desire blossomed within her. Just having him next to her was not enough. Lifting her hips, she positioned his head at the entrance and lowered her hips slightly. Instead of allowing him full entrance, she waited and tightened the muscles inside her. Supay could not take the teasing anymore and pulled violently against the restraints. As he pulled, he thrust his pelvis harshly against hers and forcefully entered her body. Above him, Phoebe gasped as waves of pleasure started to wash over her body. Struggling to keep him inside of her, she reached behind her to undo his legs before undoing his arms. Freed at last, Supay grabbed her by her hips and threw her on the bed. Pinning Phoebe's arms above her head, he thrust over and over in succession. Each thrust delved deeply into her body and pierced her core with increased pleasure. Moaning in anticipation, Phoebe began to orgasm moments before Supay joined her. Pushing into her with one last, violent thrust, he exploded within her.

Falling to the bed, Supay wrapped his arm around Phoebe and kissed her shoulder. As the heat of passion left him, he vaguely wondered what it was that she had been thinking about before sex. Weariness began to cloud his mind, and he put the matter aside until a later time.

Chapter Two

The sound of the whip whistled through the air before the harsh sting arrived. Bound against the wall, Juno struggled not to show the pain that she felt. It had only been two hours into the interrogation and she was already starting to feel the stress. She was determined not to give in to Cleonae or betray Apollo at all. In reality, it would not bother her to give away the Romans' defense preparations or military plans. What mattered to her was protecting Apollo from retribution or harm from monsters like Cleonae. Beyond just protecting Apollo, she wanted to prove to Cleonae that she could not be broken.

Stepping away from Juno, Cleonae ran the side of the whip along his finger. In normal life, he had to prevent his natural urges from taking control. The rise of the infighting among the daemons had been a delightful opportunity for him to become who he really was. Cleonae stepped back from Juno. Although the whip was enjoyable for him, he still needed to ask her questions. If he did not at least attempt to interrogate her, he would be in trouble with Phoebe.

"So, Juno. Tell me, where are the Roman daemons at? What type of preparations have they made so far?" Not waiting for her response, Cleonae whistled merrily under his breath and turned back to his table. A long knife was on the table that gleamed menacingly in the light. Picking it up, Cleonae began sharpening it. As the sharpening stone slid along the blade, cool metallic sounds rang out in the dungeon. He glanced up. Juno's face was impassive and her eyes seemed to stare through him. Her hollow gaze excited him. This woman would be one of the most difficult hostages to break ever. He grinned maliciously and set down the stone. "Well, Juno? You never responded," he growled.

Juno shook her head. "You don't care if I respond. We both know that you enjoy this task. Get it over with." With that, she closed her mouth again. Her body stiffened in preparation for his blow. Within seconds, a harsh slap hit her face resoundingly. The pain sent jolts of agony through her mind and she could barely see. How long had she been here? How much longer could she hold out? Everything seemed questionable at this point.

Struggling to bring his emotions back under control, Cleonae's veiled smile hid a depth of darkness that few had ever seen. Unfortunately, Juno was quickly becoming one of the only people in the world to see who he really was. Rubbing his knuckles absentmindedly, Cleonae reached for the knife. He stepped toward her menacingly. Despite her attempt at remaining emotionless, Juno's eyes clouded over briefly with fear. She had no clue how far he would take his 'interrogation'.

Raising the knife upwards, Cleonae reached forward quickly with his left hand and grabbed her hair. In a swift motion, he cut the entirety of her long, sleek hair off. The remaining hair was jagged and shorn just past her earlobes. Shocked, Juno trembled. She had expected something far worse than this, but the shorter hair struck a deep blow to her vanity. As Cleonae watched her tremble, he smiled. He had found a way of getting to her. Now, he just had to figure out a way to capitalize on it.

The sudden opening of the dungeon door surprised Juno and Cleonae. Phoebe entered the room without announcing herself. Glancing around the room, Phoebe barely managed to hide her shock. When she had given Cleonae the task of interrogation, she had never realized what he would do. She motioned toward the door. "Wrap up your things, Cleonae. It's my turn to interrogate the woman." Cleonae started to respond, but another warning glance from Phoebe sent him packing.

After Cleonae cleared out of the room, Phoebe shut the door. Sinking against the wall, she heaved a sigh and rubbed her temples. "I don't think you realize how many times I have wished that I could go back to my life before I was a daemon." She stared off into space wistfully. "There are few places that I have ever felt at home, and my fortune teller's shop was certainly one of them."

From across the room, Juno eyed Phoebe cautiously. She was still chained to the wall, but she did not want to ask to be let down until she knew Phoebe's true feelings. Was this a trap? An extended punishment for ruining Phoebe's life? Juno had no clue who to trust or what to believe in.

Phoebe rested her head against the wall behind her. Staring at the ceiling, she shrugged. "This is where the infighting and impending war have brought us. A man who was supposed to interrogate you turns out to be more monstrous than I ever thought." She glanced up at Juno's shorn hair. "How badly has he hurt you?"

Juno shrugged. "Other than my hair, he has only bruised me. Everything should heal in time." She motioned toward her bound hands. "Could you take these chains off?"

For once, Phoebe did not waste time with second-guessing Juno's intentions. She had completely forgotten that the chains were still on Juno and shamefully rushed to unbind her. Finally free, Juno rubbed her wrists. Even with her hair cut short and bruises hidden under her clothing, she retained a confident, unusual beauty. Juno looked Phoebe in the eyes. "I don't know how to thank you. I don't suppose there is a way for you to keep the monster away?" she asked.

Phoebe shook her head. "No, I really don't think so. I ought to make him leave the fortress or put him on construction detail. Unfortunately, there aren't many people who can control him. He's just too strong. Having him here is basically making a deal with the devil." She sighed. "As much as I have hated you for everything that you have done, I cannot allow his behavior. I truly apologize."

Cautiously, Juno tried to frame her thoughts. "If you feel so terrible, why don't you just let me go?"

"I can't. You are too dangerous and untrustworthy. Even if you did give us information, we'd have to figure out if it was one of your elaborate works of mischief. For us, this is the best place for you." Sadly, Phoebe rubbed Juno's shoulder.

Juno closed her eyes tightly. She could not stay here forever. She needed to let Apollo know that she was here and that she wanted to return back to him. "But what about Cleonae? He isn't going to stop, you know." Perhaps logic would work with Phoebe.

Phoebe paused and thought for a moment. Cleonae wouldn't stop his 'interrogations', and Phoebe could not condone that. The only way she would be able to keep Juno safe would be to get help. Supay was a shape shifter. He could turn into a lion or an animal stronger than Cleonae. If she told Supay, he would know that she had hidden away Juno and not told him. Phoebe sighed. "I will let Supay know. We can't get rid of Cleonae because we need every daemon possible on our side. There just really aren't enough daemons left in this world to support a battle like this. Each one must be kept alive to ensure that our people live on. We will need to find a way to protect you without having to actually harm or kill Cleonae." She sighed again and stood up. "One of the guards will bring you food later and some toiletries, so that you can clean up. I will let Supay know and tell the guards to get me immediately if Cleonae comes back."

Chapter Three

Juno stayed awake all night. Although she did not want to let Cleonae know of her fear, the truth was that she was frightened of his potential return. She placed herself in the corner of the room so that she could easily see the door. Curled into a ball, she tried to stay awake. Despite her best efforts, she dozed for minutes at a time throughout the night.

At some point, she must have actually fallen asleep. Although the dungeon was as dark as ever, she could hear the Greek daemons stirring within the fortress. By the sounds of it, morning was quickly turning into noon. In front of her, a pile of toiletries and food had been left. She must have slept more soundly than she thought this morning. Picking up a hairbrush and a mirror, Juno looked at her hair. It wouldn't look so bad once she trimmed the jagged ends. Finding a pair of scissors, she went to work on her hair. When that was complete, she used the bucket of water provided to sponge bath and rinse out her shortened hair. Phoebe had been more than generous last night, and some makeup had been left behind with a pile of clothes. Shrugging off her well-worn attire, Juno dressed quickly. As she applied cover up to her bruises, she began to look like her normal self again. At least things were beginning to look up, she told herself.

Finding a book amid the pile of items, Juno settled down to read. Before long, she heard another knock at the door. Curious, she told the mysterious visitor to come in. The guards, Phoebe and Cleonae never knocked, so the visitor must be someone new. As the door opened, she gasped. Phoebe had kept her word. The person standing before her was Supay. Without meaning to, Juno cast a glance of admiration in his direction. In this darkened dungeon, Supay's good looks were a welcome contrast.

Entering the room, Supay glanced around at everything within it. The bucket of bath water and questionable food were noticed immediately before he turned to look at Juno. "What happened to your hair?" he asked.

Juno shrugged and tried to appear like her normal siren self. "Cleonae. It happens."

Supay stepped forward and held out his arms silently. Even with the time that stood between now and their youthful dalliances, he knew how much her hair meant to her. Without question, Juno allowed herself to be held in his arms. His manly scent emanated from every fold of his clothing and she breathed in deeply. Although she was happy with Apollo and may love him in time, it did not erase the feelings she had once held for Supay.

Stepping back, she sat down upon the bench and crossed her legs delicately. "So did Phoebe tell you what was going on?" she queried.

Nodding darkly, Supay sank down onto the bench next to her. "Yes, she did. I wasn't particularly... pleased... that she chose not to tell me about this. You have a way of getting under people's skin." He glanced over at Juno. "What do you want me to do now? Obviously, we can't let you remain near Cleonae. He's marked you as one of his damsels and will never let you go... he is more animal than daemon half the time."

"Why don't you just let me go?" In response, Supay snorted derisively before Juno continued on. "No, really. I can't actively be involved in the fighting because of my promise to you. I'm just causing trouble here—though this time, it isn't even my fault. Wouldn't it be easier to just let me leave?" Juno fell silent and waited for Supay to respond.

Standing up, Supay began pacing the room. It was impossible to have her here or let her go. Although... he thought for a moment. While she was stuck here, she would be forced to do anything he wanted in trade. He turned to face Juno. "Okay, we will figure out a way to let you go free. Consider this a trade—and I get to decide on what is traded this time."

Swallowing hard, Juno nodded. There were many things that he could ask for, but she would not be able to offer them all... especially if he wanted her to betray the Roman daemons position or weapons.

Supay released his breath. He hadn't realized that he had been holding it as he waited for her answer. Breathing in deeply, he sat down on the floor in front of Juno so that he could see her eyes. "I'll figure out some kind of plan to get you out. First, you need to tell me the truth."

Juno stared at him blankly. "About what?"

"Everything. I want to know why I didn't see you after we were together for so long. I want you to tell me why the next time I saw you, you were with another man in a place that you knew I worked at. Tell me everything. I don't care anymore why you did the things that you did. All I want is a reason and be honest."

Closing her eyes, Juno tried to control her breathing. Her chest rose and fell rapidly as she tried to calm her mind. She had never wanted him to find out any of this, but she needed to escape from here. "Okay, I will. For the first question, the answer is that I was pregnant. My mother, Circe, told me to get rid of the father."

Supay's eyes widened. "We have a child? Where is it? How am I still alive—and what did you do with our child?"

Juno shrugged sadly. "I don't know. Circe took her. Sirens are never allowed to love and our children are raised by other sirens. It's thought to increase our bonds to each other." She sighed. "I disagree with all of that, but I didn't have a choice. Circe was perfectly fine with killing our daughter and you, so I had to go along with it."

"And me? How am I still here?"

Subconsciously, Juno backed away from him. She knew he would be angry to find out. "I did everything I could to stop it. You have to understand how I thought at the time. I loved you more than anything in the world and couldn't bear the idea of something happening to you. To protect you, I lied. Since I didn't know very many men… or any, really… there was only one real person for me to name."

Supay thought for a moment. He had never heard her mention any men when they were together. Even he had only talked about men like his father and brother. It dawned on him in an instant. Pushing her into the wall, his hands found a place around her neck. With difficulty, he kept his words even as he held her. "You were responsible for my brother."

Juno nodded meekly.

"This entire time, I thought that it was my fault. In reality, it was you." He let her go and sank down against the wall. Memories of the night with Yossele flooded his mind. Afterward, he had nightmares for years that reminded him of his brother's death.

Ragged breaths rose from Supay's body as his chest heaved. With everything that had happened over the last few years, it was difficult to handle this new development. Minutes ticked by and his breathing gradually began to slow. Next to him, Juno crouched down and began to rub his back comfortingly. He looked over at her and recognized real pity in her eyes. It was at this moment that he realized it was the truth. "So you were responsible for everything. Everything.

You never told me this. I've never even met our daughter."

Juno pulled his head onto her shoulder and kissed his forehead. "I am sorry. If you knew what Circe and her sisters are like, you would have stayed quiet as well. Driving you away and giving up our daughter was the only way to placate the other sirens. I've always loved you. Every day since then, I have tried to figure out a way to make things right and return to that time of innocence."

Looking up at her, Supay paused. He could not imagine what to say to her. Everything was suddenly starting to make sense. The last few years of his life were caused by his naiveté involving sirens. As he gazed into Juno's eyes, he saw the regret and love that still existed within them. He shook his head. His naiveté about sirens was for other sirens. Juno had always tried to act in his best interest, even if her methods were questionable.

For several moments, they sat in silence. After minutes spent in reflection, a sudden thought caused Supay to laugh silently. He smelled jasmine. Somehow, after all this time and in a dungeon, she still smelled enticingly of jasmine. Turning toward her again, he saw something new in her eyes. Desire. He groaned inwardly. After his personal experiences with her, he knew how impossible it was to stop a siren from fulfilling their desires. Worse still, he did not know if he could control his own urges. Despite everything that they had been through, he still felt inexplicably attracted to this woman. Her curves and slender figure was perfectly shaped for his hands to grab her around her waist.

Supay tried to focus on something else. Upstairs somewhere, the mother of his child waited. Instead of dimming his sudden desire, it only increased it. Nothing had been going right with Phoebe. Beyond the fact that she could not love him completely, they had grown apart on their own. Perhaps, they had never really been meant for each other. With a groan, Supay's attention was immediately drawn back to the present. Juno had placed her delicate hand upon his leg. Hearing his groan, she looked up quickly at him. He wanted her and she knew it. After weeks of being cooped up in the dungeon, Juno was in desperate need of a release. She leaned forward until her lips were just next to his. Neither person moved in for a kiss. Instead, they sat with their lips just a hair away from each other. Supay could feel her breath circulating from her mouth and sense the heat of her body. In spite of his desire to stay faithful, his cock moved with a mind of its own. It twitched and hardened in anticipation for what was to come.

Unable to move away from her, Supay used every ounce of his willpower to remain in place. Next to him, Juno tried to do the same thing. Finally, she gave up. "Look, as long as we don't follow through, it doesn't really count." Supay looked at her in confusion. She ran her finger down the front of his chest and he shivered. "Watch."

Straddling his body, Juno allowed her lips to stay centimeters off of his body. Keeping the invisible, miniscule barrier between them, she ran her teeth next to his neckline and along his clavicle. Supay placed his hands on her hips and pulled her against his body. After so long apart, it felt like his body instantly remembered Juno. He became harder than he ever imagined, as he thought about what lay within her skirt. On top of him, Juno struggled against her better self. She moved her hips against his, but kept her clothes on in a vain attempt to keep the situation from worsening. Each movement of her hips brought Supay closer and closer to orgasm without ever entering her body.

Groaning, Supay finally gave in. It was impossible to stop himself as he ripped her panties off of her body. Thrusting his cock inside her, he allowed the intense pleasure to flood his mind. This is how life should be, he thought. Each memory of their early romance flooded back into his mind as he opened his body and soul to her. Moving against the hard contours of his flesh, Juno arched her back in pleasure. She did not want to orgasm yet, but she couldn't control it. Her pent up desire had reached a breaking point. Juno tried to muffle a scream of pleasure as she started to orgasm. A white, vivid light entered her mind and took away every thought. Instead of thinking, her mind was filled with an ecstasy and nothingness that topped any orgasm she ever had. It felt like her orgasm was life itself flooding through her spirit and imbuing her with an immense vitality. Beneath her, Supay threw his head back as the same feeling surged through his soul. Between them, it felt like a wave of energy was being exchanged that was both spiritual and completely natural.

Leaning back against the wall, Supay remained inside of Juno. Exhausted, he glanced at her figure appreciatively. Her skin glowed and the scent of desire exuded from every pore. He smiled slightly. "So you really did love me, then?"

Falling against his chest, Juno ran her fingers lazily along his arm. "Yes, I did. I've always loved you."

Holding her close to his body, Supay pressed his face into her sable colored hair. "You never make things easy, do you Juno?" She shook her head in response. "I have a daughter now with Phoebe. Our relationship may be falling to pieces, but our daughter deserves two parents."

Juno looked up at Supay and the expression on her face made his heart break. Quietly, she murmured, "We have a daughter, too. I just don't know how to find her."

Supay sighed. "I know. I know. What is her name by the way? Did she look as beautiful as you?" He held her closer.

Shyly, Juno smiled. "She looked somewhat like me, but she had her father's eyes. Her name is Maia."

Kissing her forehead, Supay gently moved Juno off of his body. He zipped his pants and turned awkwardly toward her. "Look, I am still keeping my promise. I'll find a way to get you out of here safely, but I need a day or two to figure out a way to do it without having to kill Cleonae. We need all the daemons we can get." Reaching out for her hand, Supay kissed each finger individually. "I have no clue what to do about us. Before we can even get to that—or figure out where to find our daughter—we have to get you safely away." He turned and walked toward the door. With his hand on the door, he paused. Quietly, Supay spoke without looking back. "I loved you, too."

-The End-

If you enjoyed this title, I would appreciate your leaving a review of the book. Good reviews encourage an author to write as well as help books to sell. Good reviews can be just a few short sentences describing what you liked about the book without having a spoiler. If you could spend 30 seconds writing a review, I would appreciate it: you can review this title right now at your favorite retailer.

Here is a preview of **another story** you may enjoy:

Romeo Alpha: A BBW Paranormal Shifter Romance - Book 1

AMANDA WONDERED how the hell she had gotten so far away from home. When she walked, she usually didn't go past a couple of blocks, but she felt so different today. Something was pushing her further and in a different direction, and she wasn't sure what it was. But she didn't care at the moment, because she just wanted to walk.

Not thinking twice about where she was going, she let her gut instinct give her the direction she needed.

Her grandmother had always told her to go with her gut. She'd said human instinct was better than anything. "Intuition is a girl's best friend," she would say, and then they would both laugh. Talks she and her grandmother had always seemed to pop into her head at the strangest of times, like now.

Here she was, going for a walk, and wondering why she wanted to go in a different direction, and there was her grandmother's voice in her head, propelling her along. Amanda missed her grandmother more with every passing year.

Amanda paused and thought about her life thus far. She had just graduated from college and started working in the local animal hospital, but it wasn't quite like she had thought. She didn't see the care and passion she'd hoped to find in the industry. In the city, being a vet was all about how much money you could make, how many pets you could treat. And, at twenty-four, it was hard to be taken seriously.

Her two female roommates were nice, but they all just went their separate ways. They didn't eat ice cream and watch movies like on *Friends*. They didn't share secrets or even laugh or hang out. They really just slept in the same apartment, and they usually weren't even home at the same time. Except Amanda, that is.

Amanda was always at home, it seemed. She had nowhere else to go, really. The other two girls spent most nights out with their real friends or their boyfriends. Amanda lived a lonely life, but she was happy. At least, she was pretty sure she was happy. After all, she had an upstanding career, and she still had money left over from her savings.

Both her parents had been killed in a car accident years ago. Amanda had graduated from high school with no family there that day or on the day she graduated from college. It was what it was, though, and she knew that her parents watched her from Heaven.

The only positive thing was that her parents had been prepared and had made sure they left enough money and a big enough life insurance policy to help her out. They would be surprised but happy knowing how much that money had helped her in the years after their death. She was proud to say that she was able to live off of it through her college years. She'd never even had to get a job like most kids did. Amanda had been able to focus on her classes.

That freedom wasn't worth it, though. She would have worked three jobs at a time while going to school for one more day with her parents.

However, the account was finally starting to dry up, and she needed to think about what she would do. Sure, she had a new job that could pay her bills, but those loans were piling up with interest. Even a vet job only went so far.

Amanda sighed as she began the trek back toward the house.

Amanda liked her walks in the evening. It helped her to relax, enjoying the quiet time alone. And while Amanda wasn't overweight by any means, it helped slim her waistline, which showed those extra biscuits she liked every now and again.

She turned and began to make her way back to the townhouse she shared with her roommates, but stopped as she heard a noise

A rustling came from behind her, and she turned to see the bushes shaking. Looking over to the other side of the sidewalk, she saw those bushes shake as well. Not wanting to wait around to find out what was behind the leaves, she took off at a run. She swore she heard a growl come from behind her, but she didn't turn to see what was chasing her. That would only slow her down. As she reached the door to her home, she quickly turned the knob and went through headfirst. Shutting the door quickly, she looked out the window. She got a glimpse of a long black furry tail as something ran around to the side of her building.

"What in the world are you doing, Amanda?" Betsy stood there looking at her inquisitively.

"Something was chasing me."

"What?"

"I don't know what it was, but something big and furry was chasing me. I saw a long black tail just now when I walked into the house."

"You mean when you dove into the house?" Betsy's grin faded. "I'll call the game warden. If there is a big animal outside, then none of us need to go out there until they find it and get rid of it."

"Well, I don't want them to kill it."

"I know, silly, but if it's a wild animal, they can take it out to the National Forest and let it loose. The city is no place for a wild animal." Betsy turned and picked up the phone from the receiver.

Amanda stood in shocked silence as she listened to her roommate tell the person on the other end of the phone what had happened.

She knew from Betsy's tone that she and the person on the other end of the phone were questioning her sanity. They lived in a big city, and the closest thing they got to a wild animal was a stray cat or two. They didn't even get raccoons. If there was some huge animal like she thought, then it would make headline news.

Shaking her head in aggravation, Amanda turned toward her room. She suddenly felt silly and didn't want to have to explain what she saw to any more people.

"Amanda? Where are you going? They are on their way and might need to talk to you."

"Tell them it was a dog. Now that I'm thinking about it, it kind of looked like that couple that lives down the road's greyhound. Maybe he just got out."

"Are you sure, Amanda?" Betsy asked, turning and saying something into the phone.

Without saying another word, Amanda shut the door to her room tight and then quickly locked the door. She looked over her room and, seeing the window open and the curtains blowing in the breeze, she ran over to push the window pane down and lock it tight. As she stood there, she looked out into the woods that made up her backyard. There, in the distance, two yellow eyes stared back at her.

Suddenly, more eyes appeared, and it seemed the animals went on forever. She was amazed, since the woods behind her house were very dense and small. The dark night was lit with a full moon. A shiver raced through her as she stood there and stared into the first set of yellow eyes. She quickly shut the curtains and went to sit on her bed. She didn't think she would ever be able to fall asleep knowing what was out there. As she laid her head on the pillow, her mind wondered to large beasts with yellow eyes and sharp fangs. But she was soon fast asleep.

Amanda awoke with a yawn. It had been almost a month since the incident with what she now called a dog. She had agreed with Betsy that her mind had been playing tricks on her that night. There were often times when she was sure she felt eyes on her, and she would turn in one direction or another, looking. What she was seeking, she didn't know, but somewhere in the back of her mind, she just wanted to know if the eyes she had seen that night had been real or just part of her dreams that evening. She was still so uneasy about it that her walks seemed to get earlier and earlier each evening.

She was just about to walk out the door when her phone started ringing. She quickly grabbed it and pushed the button to answer it.

"Hello."

"Ms. Walker?"

"Yes?"

"Hello, Ms. Walker, my name is Ernest Montgomery. I am calling to tell you that your aunt has passed away."

"My aunt? But I don't have any family. You must have the wrong Ms. Walker."

"No, ma'am. Your father was Joshua Walker, correct? Mother Maureen Walker?"

"Yes."

"Then, I have the right Ms. Walker. It is your father's sister I am referring to. She unexpectedly passed away from a heart attack. I am very sorry for your loss."

"Oh, my gosh! I never knew I even had any family. I am very sad that I didn't get to meet her."

"Yes, ma'am. I'm sure. She was a nice woman. I have also called you to see if you can meet with me. I need to go over her will with you."

"Her will?"

"Yes, ma'am. Your aunt was a wealthy woman."

"Oh? Um, okay. When would you like to meet?"

"The sooner, the better."

"Okay. How about today?"

"That would be great. I am in Slatesville, in the valley. "

"Oh. Okay. That is just forty-five minutes from me. I can be there in a couple of hours."

"Sounds good, ma'am. I am at the *Montgomery Law Firm*. I am the only attorney in the town."

"Okay. Thank you, sir. I will see you soon."

"Yes, ma'am. I'll be waiting."

Amanda fell back on the couch, stunned, for what seemed like forever. Everything was pushed to the back of her mind as she thought about what she had just learned. She had a family. Well, she *did* have a family. Now her aunt was gone. Could there be others in her family who she knew nothing about? She didn't know, but she did know one thing. She wasn't going to find out sitting around here, twiddling her thumbs. She needed to get going fast.

Amanda headed for the kitchen. She wasn't surprised to see that no one was there. Of course her roommates weren't home. They were either in class or with their boyfriends.

Smiling, she made a cup of coffee and drank it slowly, thinking about what she might find out. Then, with a deep sigh, she made her way to her car. She looked at the small Honda with pride. It was a pile of junk to some, but it held a special place in her heart. She hadn't been able to get rid of her father's car. Instead, she had sold her own.

She looked down at the small picture he had taped to the dash near the speedometer. She was about six in the picture, and she had been holding her mom's cheeks in her hands as she kissed her.

She remembered the day like it was yesterday. They had just got to a cabin they vacationed in. She had enjoyed herself so much. The little cabin had one bedroom with a queen-sized bed where her parents slept and a set of bunk beds for her. They had stayed up late roasting marshmallows as her father told her scary stories about wolves and vampires. She had ended up in their bed, snuggled between the two of them. They had spent the next day hiking and walking trails and seeing tons of waterfalls and animals.

She had loved it and had never forgotten. It soon became a family tradition to go camping every year. After some of those trips, they didn't return home.

Instead, they moved on to a different location. The constant moving had been hard on her as a kid, but she would have never told her parents that. She had felt like they were hiding something from her. Of course, she had been young back then and had blown it off as childhood curiosity. Now, with this new family member, she wasn't so sure.

Her parents had been very quiet people. They seemed cautious of everything going on around them and were even a little jumpy at times. Maybe there was more going on here than she thought. She needed to find out.

She wiped away a tear and go in the car. The car had a huge dent in one side and was almost fifteen years old, but it got her where she needed to go. She slid the car into drive and smiled to herself.

"Dad would be proud that his car was still running so good, wouldn't he, Trixy?" She and her father had named the car together.

Amanda turned onto the next road and made her way down the narrow two-lane road that led into the mountains. She had never been this way because her parents always went the long way around the mountains. They said they liked to take the scenic route.

She came to a small wooden sign that said *Slatesville—Welcome to your home away from home*. She smiled at the welcoming sign and kept on her way to the town. As she drove, she was amazed at how beautiful everything was. The low-hanging branches of the trees scraped the roof of the car every once in a while.

She was amazed at how many animals she saw. Deer acted as if they weren't afraid of her car. Raccoons were plentiful, and she jumped when a large black snake slithered across the road. There were people all around, and they watched her car curiously as she made her way down the street.

The town reminded her of a long lost western ghost town. It was a little spooky, and she caught herself checking the doors to make sure they were locked. The men nodded at her as she moved forward and many of the people smiled, although they held themselves back a little.

Amanda finally saw the sign that said *Montgomery Law Firm*. She pulled into one of the many vacant parking spots and slowly got out of the car. A handsome man leaned against the building she was about to enter. His brown eyes had flecks of yellow and orange in their deep depths. She smiled slightly, and the man just continued to stare as he looked her over slowly.

"Can I help you, ma'am?"

"I am just here to see Mr. Montgomery."

"Well, you're in the right place, Miss…?"

"Oh, Amanda. Amanda Walker. And you are?"

Something changed in his eyes as he smiled at her and made his way to her side. He held out his hand to her. "Name's Curtis Livingston."

"Oh. Do you live here?"

"Yes. I'm one of the controlling partners here in Slatesville. Well, I have to be going. It was good to meet you."

"You, too, Mr. Livingston."

"Please, call me Curt. Everyone does."

"Only if you call me Amanda."

"That's a deal, sweet lady." She flushed all over when he raised her hand to his lips and gently caressed her knuckles with a brief touch of his mouth. She felt the rise in temperature in her cheeks spread across her upper chest. She stood there and watched as he walked away from her down the street to slip inside a store. She felt foolish and realized that she had been staring. She shook her head, trying to think straight and clear the thoughts that were running through her mind.

Amanda was always aware that she wasn't the Barbie doll type of girl. Although she wasn't fat, she wasn't rail thin, which most men liked, either. Her waist and stomach didn't look like a washboard, although it didn't look like a bunch of bread dough either.

She instantly felt inadequate and quickly turned around to walk to the door of the attorney's office. Knocking, she was surprised when the door instantly opened. The man who opened the door wasn't what she expected. Mr. Montgomery was a short, pudgy man. He didn't wear a business suit, and he didn't seem stuffy at all. He was older and had a short goatee around his mouth. His hair was pulled back into a ponytail at the back of his neck, and he smiled when he saw her.

"You must be Amanda. You look just like your father, except for your eyes. You have your mother's eyes. Let's hope you didn't inherit your father's temper, though," he chuckled.

"You knew my father?"

"Oh, why yes, my dear. We grew up together, Josh and I. Have to say we got into a lot of trouble as kids, and your aunt Mabel was always there to wag her finger and tell on us. You see, there were the three of us; Joshua, Jeremiah, and I. We were called the three musketeers. Mabel wanted to be the fourth, but you know boys. We would never let her, so she always ran and told on us to get back at us for not including her; the little minx." He told the story fondly, and she instantly knew that this man held her family in the highest regard. She also knew he was her ticket to finding out the truth about her family.

"Do I have any more family that I don't know of?" She held her breath, as though she were a child again, asking if Santa Claus was real.

"I am sure you do, my dear. Unfortunately, your aunt was the last of your father's line. She couldn't have any children, and most of the family was killed in a fire in '90. I am sure there is still family on your mother's side, though. However, I must warn you that they are not the kind of people you want to know. Now, if you will come in, I will tell you about everything that now belongs to you."

"What?"

"Oh, my dear, you must know that your father's family had a legacy. You are the only Traverse left to take over the family business."

"What? I don't know what you're talking about."

"They never did tell you who you really are, did they? Oh, you poor child. I am afraid you are going to learn some things about yourself that are going to be hard for you. You must still be a virgin as well."

"I beg your pardon, sir, but I don't see how that's any of your damn business."

"No, my dear, I do not mean to be crude. I was just saying that you have never undergone the Change. It will happen, though. You recently turned twenty-four, and everything changes now."

"What change? What in the hell are you talking about?"

"They hid that from you, too? Oh my gosh. You don't know? Oh, Lord. Okay, first things first. You are now the owner of your family's estate."

"Family estate? So I have a house."

He smiled kindly at her. "Not just a house, my dear. It is what holds the legacy of your family name together. The estate has fifteen bedrooms with their own bathrooms and fireplaces, a kitchen, dining room, parlor, living area, office, library, Carolina room, staff quarters, wrap-around porch with two different sections screened in, pool, tennis courts and 300 acres. It was the pride and joy of your ancestor, Edgar. He was a distant grandfather of yours."

"Oh my gosh."

"Yes, ma'am. How about this? How about I get the keys and directions to the place? You go take a look at it, and then we can talk tomorrow about what you want to do. Stephan has been looking over things, and since your aunt's death, he has given everyone time off until you arrive and decide where to go from there."

Amanda wasn't sure she had the energy to deal with all of this tonight. "Unfortunately, it is very late. Is there somewhere that I can stay for a couple days and then I can go from there and take the day tomorrow to go look at the place?"

"That is perfect. Just give me a second, and I'll find a place for you to stay tonight."

Amanda sat quietly and listened to him talk on his phone. She didn't even hear his words as she thought of what she was going to do.

"I have gotten you a little cabin to rent down the road," he said, drawing her attention back to him. "It is in the woods a little but has electricity and such. On such short notice, I couldn't find anything else. It is only about ten minutes away. The key will be under the mat at the front door. Just go on in and make yourself at home."

"That is perfect. Thank you so much."

"You're welcome, my dear, and we will talk tomorrow. Say ten o'clock tomorrow morning? We will meet here and go to see the house together."

"Perfect. Thank you, Mr. Montgomery."

If you enjoyed this sample then look for **Romeo Alpha: A BBW Paranormal Shifter Romance - Book 1.**

Here is a preview of **another story** you may also enjoy:

True Lovers - The Leather Satchel Romance Series, Book 6

VALTINA AND Demetri sat silently under the willow tree, anxiously awaiting Ladaya's return. They'd stopped trying to guess how much time had passed since Ladaya returned to The Afterlife; they were now marking the time by the number of wraiths Demetri had slaughtered. So far, the warrior had eliminated five of the monsters. Valtina had known that their sanctuary had been breached, but it hadn't seemed real until she saw the first black hooded creature emerge from the dense grey fog. As time passed, Valtina became more and more nervous; she knew that in this situation, no news was not good news.

Demetri stiffened, and Valtina followed his gaze. Another wraith was approaching from the fog. As the warrior rose to confront the monster, the tip of a silver dagger broke through its chest, and it evaporated where it stood. Ladaya and a spirit Valtina didn't recognize stood before them.

"Ladaya!" Valtina exclaimed, "I was starting to worry!"

"Hello, August." Demetri nodded to the other spirit. August nodded in reply. Demetri continued. "Valtina, this is August, my General. I take it no one is traveling alone now?" he asked, turning to the Generals.

"It's nice to meet you, Valtina. I've heard wonderful things," August began. He turned to Demetri. "No, we've all been instructed to travel with a partner. The wraiths are flooding Middle World, and we believe they're looking for a way in to The Afterlife."

Ladaya watched panic spread over Valtina's face. "Don't worry child," she assured her. "We've learned of a way to defeat them. There's lore of a weapon, a sword forged in the fires of the Underworld that will destroy the wraith army. If the Queen is decapitated with the sword, the entire army will evaporate. They're all connected, you see…" Ladaya trailed off.

"Are we sure the weapon exists?" Demetri asked with an air of doubt. "I mean, lore isn't always reliable."

"We're pretty confident," August answered. "The rest of the lore regarding wraiths has proved true. We have no reason to think the sword is any different."

"So, do you know where it is?" Valtina asked. "Let us help, we can search with the other spirits."

Ladaya smiled. "Once again, I appreciate your offer, and your dedication… but we all have specific jobs to do, and your next mission is the most important to date. Other spirits, whose gifts are suited to the mission, are searching for the sword."

"Ladaya, speaking of weapons…" Valtina began, but was interrupted by her General.

"I know, Valtina," Ladaya sighed. "You want a weapon. As well you should, knowing that Morgonda is targeting you. And at this point, I'd give you a dagger if

I could. But I don't believe it would do you much good."

"Why not?" Valtina asked.

"Demetri," Ladaya turned to the warrior, "would you be so kind as to let Valtina hold your dagger for a moment?"

Nodding in confusion, Demetri held his dagger out to Valtina. The moment she touched the weapon, her hand burned in pain. Gasping, she pulled away.

"Ouch!" she cried. "I can't even touch it?!"

"No," Ladaya sighed, "Valtina, your spirit is composed of pure love. The weapon, and its purpose, is in direct conflict with your spirit force, making it impossible for you to hold it."

Valtina was disappointed; she also wished Ladaya had told her that the first time she'd asked for a weapon. It would have saved her a lot of frustration. But the fog continued to grow denser, and Valtina knew that she must stay focused on her mission. "Ok, so I can't protect myself. Where are we going next?" she asked with a slight tone of defeat.

"Las Vegas," Ladaya answered. "We've learned of a dire situation there. I'm sending you to a young woman named Penelope. Her father was a non-denominational minister who worked to help the souls of Sin City. Six years ago, the preacher made a drastic change in his ministry and began preaching vehemently against 'sins of the flesh'. He brainwashed his congregation to believe that even marital sex can bring evil into the home, and should only be indulged in for the purpose of procreation. The result of these ministries has been a sharp decrease in the number of soul-mates pairing up. They believe that their natural sexual attraction goes against God, and that the person they belong with is the person they are LEAST physically attracted to."

If you enjoyed this sample then look for **True Lovers - The Leather Satchel Romance Series, Book 6.**

Here is a preview of **another story** you may enjoy:

Fifty Recipes For Disaster: A New Adult Romance Series - Book 1 by Carla Coxwell

"**ALL RIGHT**, chefs, you have ninety seconds to get your food plated and presented. If your dish isn't ready, you will automatically be eliminated."

My cooking instructor, Chef Michelle Lee, walks through the room, examining our stations. My fellow cooking students and I are competing for the chance to enter another competition. The winner of today's cooking challenge will get the chance to compete for a full-time apprenticeship at Fission, one of Austin's hottest restaurants.

I'm not confident in many aspects of my life, but I know I dominate in the kitchen. I begin plating my dish just as Chef Lee approaches my station.

"Your food presents beautifully as usual, Kiara," she tells me with a smile. "If it tastes as good as it looks, you've got this in the bag," she adds with a soft whisper.

The instructors at *Le Cordon Bleu College of Culinary Arts* aren't supposed to show favoritism to their students, but Chef Lee keeps a soft spot for me. Along with being one of my teachers, she's also my faculty adviser, and she knows the unusual circumstances that brought me to the school.

"Time's up," she calls out to the class. "Place your finished plates on the head table."

I walk my plate to the front of the room and place it on top of the placard that holds my student ID number. My classmates follow suit… several of them glare at me after looking at my dish. I am delighted, knowing they're all both jealous and impressed I was able to execute a well-developed *Cioppino* within the given time frame. My rich seafood stew is accompanied by fresh sourdough loaves. I examine my classmates' dishes and feel my chances of winning are good.

"Clear away your stations," Chef Lee directs. "Chef Lawton will be here shortly to judge your plates, and I don't want any evidence of who made what on display when he arrives."

Chef Lawton is the *sous* chef at Fission and the judge of this stage of the apprenticeship competition. I clear my station quickly and then I take a seat at the front of the room. I want to be able to see Chef Lawton's expressions as he tastes each dish.

As I sit nervously in my chair, my classmates finish clearing their stations. I can tell everyone else is just as anxious as I am… we've received plenty of critiques from our instructors but this will be the first time a professional chef from a restaurant will be tasting our food. The door of the classroom opens and a tall man wearing a black chef's jacket enters the room.

"Chef Lawton, it's so lovely to see you," Chef Lee welcomes him. "I can't tell you how excited we are to participate in this competition."

"We're excited as well," Chef Lawton replies. "We're always looking for new, innovative chefs at

Fission. I'm looking forward to tasting the dishes and welcoming one of your students into the final leg of the competition. I see that all of the plates are ready. If it's all right with you, I'll get started."

"Of course," Chef Lee agrees.

I try not to hold my breath as I watch Chef Lawton sample each of the plates. I feel encouraged when he reaches mine. Instead of sampling one bite and moving on, he holds the broth in his mouth for a moment, and then tastes each type of seafood in turn. The expression on his face tells me that my stew is perfect, and I say a silent prayer I haven't been out-cooked by any of my classmates.

"First off, I'd like to say this is an impressive display," the seasoned chef begins. "Everything on this table is up to par with the level of skill and talent I expect to see from second-year students. That being said, there is a clear winner. One chef not only executed a delicious dish, but also added a few subtle, original touches that showed innovation and creativity."

Adrenaline rushes through me as he moves to stand behind my dish. "Who created this *Cioppino*?" he asks.

I blush involuntarily as I raise my hand.

"And what is your name, Chef?"

"Kiara Sands," I reply, trying to mask the excitement in my voice.

"Well, Chef Sands, it's an honor to welcome you to the next stage of the competition. I look forward to tasting more of your food as the weeks progress. I am needed back at Fission, but Chef Lee will provide you with the details of your new position." He turns to the rest of the class. "To the rest of you, don't be discouraged. You all provided me with excellent dishes, and you have bright futures ahead of you."

"Thank you, Chef," the class responds in unison.

Chef Lawton makes a quick exit, and Chef Lee takes his place behind the head table. "Excellent work today, class. You're dismissed until tomorrow," she announces. My classmates gather their things and leave the room… I stay behind to talk to Chef Lee.

"Kiara, I'm so proud of you." She beams once we are alone. "As you know, there will be two other chefs competing with you at Fission. You're the only one who's been selected from *Le Cordon Bleu*, and I know you'll represent us well." She moves to her desk and pulls a large package from her bottom drawer. "Here is your apprenticeship packet. You'll receive your Fission jacket when you report for work tomorrow morning. If you have any questions, or just need someone to talk to, you know where to reach me."

"This seems like a wonderful dream, and part of me is afraid that I'll wake up any minute now," I confess.

Chef Lee gives me a maternal smile. "This is a dream, Kiara. It's *your* dream. And you're well on your way to achieving it."

The information packet Chef Lee presented me with instructs me to be at Fission at 10:00 am. I check my dashboard clock as I pull into the parking lot… 9:40 am. I feel smug, knowing I'm probably the first of the three competitors to arrive. I check my makeup in the rear-view mirror before exiting my car.

Fission is housed in a modern brick building in East Austin, one of the city's burgeoning hipster areas. The area gives off a relaxed, laid-back vibe, but I know the kitchen of Fission will be anything but.

I push open the heavy, solid oak door and am greeted by a pixy-sized hostess with spiked, lavender hair.

"Table for one?" she asks me brightly.

"No," I reply nervously. "My name is Kiara Sands. I'm supposed to start work today."

"Oh! You're one of the newbies!" She says warmly. "I'm Megan. It's a pleasure to meet you. The other two are already here. I'll show you to their table."

Damn it! I'd been so sure I'd make the best impression by arriving first, and here I am, the last of the apprentices to report for our first day.

Megan seems to sense my disappointment. "Don't worry. Paul doesn't give a shit how early people show up. As long as you're here when you're scheduled, you'll be fine. And you haven't missed anything. The other two have just been sitting alone since they got here," she offers reassuringly.

"Thank you for that," I say half-heartedly. As I follow Megan through the restaurant, I'm struck by the eclectic, well-placed décor. All of the tables are made of the same polished oak as the front door. The water goblets on the tabletops are tinted in hues of blue, green, and rose… a selection of art from all around the world adorns the walls. The ambiance is on the right side of the fine line between cozy and overwhelming. The restaurant offers a large main dining room, with smaller, more private rooms on each side.

"This is a beautiful place," I say as Megan leads me toward the back of the main room.

"It is," she agrees. "Paul handled all of the decorating himself. He says that Austin is a melting pot, and he wants all of our customers to feel at home when they dine here."

I'm about to comment on how successfully that goal had been achieved when we arrive at a table occupied by a beautiful blonde woman and a swarthy man with sandy blond hair. A pot of coffee and three cups sit on the table.

"Kiara Sands, this is Jenny Foster and Robbs Martin," Megan introduces us. She checks her watch before speaking again. "It's a quarter to ten, so I imagine that Paul will be out shortly. I suggest you get fully caffeinated and enjoy this time off your feet. It will be the last one for today," she warns with a friendly, knowing tone.

I take a seat in the chair next to Jenny as Megan moves back to the hostess station. "It's a pleasure to meet you both," I offer.

"It's a pleasure to meet you too," Robbs replies. "Congratulations on making it this far in the competition. And I'd like to apologize right now for how thoroughly I'm going to kick both of your asses. This job is mine." He speaks with a blend of arrogance and sarcasm, and I can tell immediately that Robbs and I are not going to get along.

Personal relationships are something I struggle with. In my experience, there's no point in getting close to someone who will inevitably let you down. I prefer to keep my head down and focus on getting my job done. As Chef Lee said yesterday, I have a dream and I'm well on my way to achieving it. I'll be damned if I let Robbs or anyone else get in my way.

"Just ignore Robbs," Jenny advises me. "He thinks that he's God's gift to food... women too, probably." She giggles. "So Kiara, what's your story? Which campus were you plucked from?"

"I'm in my second year at *Le Cordon Bleu*," I answer with pride. In my opinion, *Le Cordon Bleu* is the best culinary school in the area—it's also the hardest to get in to. Jenny seems impressed by my background, but Robbs laughs and dismisses it immediately.

"The *Bleu* is all right, I guess," he snorts, "if you're happy being complacent and doing everything old-school."

"I wasn't aware that being classically trained is a bad thing," I reply shortly. "Tell me, what culinary Mecca do you hail from?"

"*Escoffier*," he answers with a cocky smile. "You know, where all of the innovative, cutting-edge people attend. Three of my instructors were nominated for the James Beard award. So like I said, no hard feelings, but I'm going to kick both of your asses. *Escoffier* specializes in farm-to-table cuisine, so I'm exactly the kind of chef Fission is looking for."

I dismiss his statement with a glare. While the *Auguste Escoffier School of Culinary Arts* is reputed for turning out fantastic chefs, in some culinary circles it's dismissed as a hipster college that prioritizes food trends over basic technique and skill.

I don't feel like debating the merits of my education with Robbs, so I turn to Jenny. "And where do you go?" I ask pleasantly.

"The Art Institute," she replies. "I'm still not positive that cooking is my life's passion. I wanted to go to a college that offers other programs, in case I decided to change my major."

"If you're not sure that you want to be a chef, then what the fuck are you doing here?" Robbs asks hotly. "You should give your spot to someone who knows that this is what they want."

Jenny's green eyes fill with both anger and embarrassment, and I can tell she's fumbling for a response.

"I don't agree with that at all," I say warmly. "What better way to find out if you enjoy working in a real kitchen, than by actually doing it?"

"That's exactly what my instructor said when I won this spot," Jenny says with a nod.

"I see how it's going to be," Robbs interjects with more sarcasm. "The two of you are going to band together in 'sisterhood' and gang up on me."

"That's not how it's going to be at all," a firm voice says from behind me. I turn to see one of the most attractive men I've ever laid my eyes on. He's tall, with broad shoulders, blue eyes, and sandy blond hair. He's also wearing a black chef's jacket, identical to the one Chef Lawton wore when he judged my dish. He holds eye contact with me for several moments before he speaks again.

"This competition will come down to one thing and one thing only... the quality of your food. Only one of you will be named my new apprentice, so ganging up on each other won't serve any purpose. I'm Paul Weston, and I'd like to welcome you to my restaurant." He extends his hand to me.

I respond with a firm handshake and a smile. "I'm Kiara Sands. Thank you for this opportunity."

"You're here because you deserve to be. No thanks are necessary," he assures me.

If you enjoyed this sample then look for **Fifty Recipes For Disaster: A New Adult Romance Series - Book 1 by Carla Coxwell**.

Other Books by Darla Dunbar

- The Romeo Alpha BBW Paranormal Shifter Romance Series

- Romeo Alpha Blood Lines Romance

- The Alpha Feud BBW Paranormal Shifter Romance Series

- The Alpha Packed BBW Paranormal Shifter Romance Series

- The Mind Talker Paranormal Romance Series

- The Leather Satchel Paranormal Romance Series

Get the latest update on new releases from the author at:

https://darladunbar.com/newsletter/

About the Author - Darla Dunbar

Darla has been interested in paranormal romance since she was a teenager in high school. It was then that she discovered she could fulfill her fantasies through her writing.

Observing people and human behavior in the area of romance has always been one of her favorite pastimes. Combining that with an overactive imagination is a sure fire way of coming up with interesting themes.

Connect with Darla Dunbar

I really appreciate you reading my book! Here are my social media coordinates:

Friend me on Facebook:
https://www.facebook.com/darladunbar/

Follow me on Twitter: https://twitter.com/DarlDunbar

Check me out on Goodreads:
https://www.goodreads.com/author/show/8425857.Darla_Dunbar

Subscribe to my newsletter:
https://darladunbar.com/newsletter/

Visit my website: https://darladunbar.com/